This book belongs to:

_____

_____

For my family near and far,
   who taught me the true value of traditions.

And to my kids,
   whom I love "the mostest!"

Text © 2021 by Danielle Marietta
Illustrations © 2021 by Masha Klot
Published in the United States of America by Books & Things Publishing.
DanielleMariettaBooks.com

ISBN 978-1-7357218-1-1

Designed by Masha Klot.

"And to all a good night!
They especially like it when I say that last little bit." Santa leaned in with a sparkle in his eye and he smiled.

And just like that, Christmas was over.
All the presents were delivered,
the milk and cookies were sampled,
and the sun was rising behind them.
With the flick of his wrist, the bells jingled
and the reindeer sped on toward the horizon
towing the sleigh behind them.

As they arrived back home,
Nick leaned in for a hug.

"Thanks, Uncle Kris! See you in the morning. Christmas is fun but my favorite tradition here is **the Holly-day After!"**

"Yes, mine too," his Uncle Kris, or Santa as some call him, agreed. "You were a great help, as always. Get some rest and I'll see you soon."

Nick hopped off the sleigh and gathered the reindeer.

He walked them back to the lodge and got them into their stalls.

Once each sleepy reindeer was tucked in under the hay, Nick climbed up the ladder to his family's loft overlooking their livestock below.

"Night," his big brother Noel mumbled as he rolled back to sleep.

"Goodnight!" his twin sisters, Joy and Grace, called out when they heard him climbing into his bed.

"And to all a goodnight!" Nick replied with a smirk.

Giggles echoed in the lodge that late Christmas night.

"Hush" said their Father Fred.

"Holly-day After is almost here. And as tradition goes, we start bright and early!"

A calming silence fell over the lodge and all of the North Pole.

As the sun arose and the fresh snow glistened, the feeling of joy filled the air. Nick, along with his brother and sisters, ran into the kitchen.

"Let the Holly-day Pancake Tower Competition begin!"

The boys had won the past two years. They knew their sisters were ready, and had been planning out their pancakes for months!

The brothers kept their work station clean
and organized, carefully laying out
their blueprints and prepping their supplies.

Joy and Grace, not so much.
They were already flipping their first pancake!
Bowls, pans, cracked egg shells
and clouds of flour floated everywhere!
But the smell of tradition blossomed
and the pancake creations
were growing.

Noel was stacking and Nick was shaping the pancakes into a giant Holly-day After tree. Holly berries sprinkled throughout like ornaments on a Christmas tree.

But the twins, oh the twins! They had created a full replica of the North Pole city center! They beamed as they took a step back to see what they had done.

"Merry Holly-day After!"

Nick and his family all cheered back.

While the younger kids played and ran everywhere,
the teenagers were busy being too cool to be silly.
The grownups were all talking in their own little world.
Nick's Father and Uncle were flipping the family crest
to see who would be Santa next year.

Nick loved this time with
everyone together.
The rest of the year is so busy with work,
but this is always one day
he can count on.

As they all gathered around the beautiful tables, love and smiling faces surrounded them. Pancakes covered in powdered sugar and warm maple syrup with extra chocolaty hot cocoa to wash it down - these were all part of the traditions he loved. With a full belly, Nick sat back and listened while others shared stories of favorite Holly-day After memories.

And then it was time. One by one, they gathered their boots, coats and hats and took the party out back.

Nick and his siblings handed out tree sprouts to all. Everyone marched out to the fields behind the lodge and picked a place to plant their future Holly-day After tree.

While they did so, they all sang,

Quiet hums mimicking the tune continued
until every last tree was planted.
This is what the day was all about.
Time spent together and time giving back.

Standing outside that chilly night,
everyone looked out to the rolling hills
of Holly-day After trees.
Some were no bigger than Nick,
but others touched the clouds.

"**The traditions** we start today can live on forever," Uncle Kris whispered.

"It's up to each of us to keep them going. Sometimes we might not all be together, but when you look out over these hills, you will be reminded of those past times together."

And with that, the day was done.
Nick, Noel, Joy and Grace squeezed everyone extra tight as they left.

"See you at school,"
the twins shouted to their classmates.

"See you in the workshop,"
Noel said to his friends.

Uncle Kris lifted Nick up onto his shoulder.
He had the same sparkle in his eye that he had the night before.
While waving goodbye to their friends and family,
they said in unison,

# Windows 10 installeren

Deze handleiding toont de installatie van Windows 10 op een nieuwe pc, dus een pc zonder een reeds geïnstalleerd besturingssysteem. Windows 10 komt als ISO-bestand. Dit bestand moet eerst op een USB-stick geplaatst worden. Om een ISO-bestand bootable op een USB-stick te kopiëren, kan er gebruik gemaakt worden van het programma Rufus.

Rufus

Rufus is een programma dat een ISO-bestand op een USB-stick kopieert en deze bootable maakt. Het programma kan gedownload worden via https://rufus.ie/. Het programma is gratis en open source.

![Rufus](rufus.png)

1. Selecteer de USB-stick waarop het ISO-bestand geplaatst moet worden.
2. Selecteer het ISO-bestand.
3. Klik op "Start" om het proces te starten.
4. Wacht tot het proces voltooid is.

Windows 10 installeren

1. Plaats de USB-stick in de pc waarop Windows 10 geïnstalleerd moet worden.
2. Start de pc op en open het bootmenu. Dit kan meestal door op F12, F11 of F2 te drukken tijdens het opstarten.
3. Selecteer de USB-stick als bootdevice.
4. Windows 10 zal nu opstarten vanaf de USB-stick.
5. Volg de stappen op het scherm om Windows 10 te installeren.

Windows 10 activeren

Na de installatie moet Windows 10 geactiveerd worden. Dit kan door een productcode in te voeren. De productcode kan gekocht worden bij Microsoft of bij een andere leverancier.

1. Open de instellingen van Windows 10.
2. Ga naar "Update en beveiliging".
3. Klik op "Activering".
4. Klik op "Productcode wijzigen".
5. Voer de productcode in en klik op "Volgende".
6. Windows 10 is nu geactiveerd.

CPSIA information can be obtained
at www.ICGtesting.com
Printed in the USA
JSHW012004190521
14953JS00005B/50